Clare

and her
Captain

*To dear Christian and John with much love
from Michael, Captain and Clare*

For Gillian and her horses – C.R.

onkers

First published in 2015 in Great Britain by
Barrington Stoke Ltd
18 Walker Street, Edinburgh, EH3 7LP

www.barringtonstoke.co.uk

This story was first published in a different form as
Thatcher Jones (Macmillan Education Ltd, 1975)

Text © 1975 Michael Morpurgo
Illustrations © 2015 Catherine Rayner

The moral right of Michael Morpurgo and Catherine Rayner
to be identified as the author and illustrator of this work
has been asserted in accordance with the Copyright,
Designs and Patents Act, 1988

A CIP catalogue record for this book is available
from the British Library upon request

ISBN: 978-1-78112-435-2

Printed in China by Leo

Michael Morpurgo

Clare
and her
Captain

With illustrations by
Catherine Rayner

Conkers

CONTENTS

CHAPTER 1
Traffic Jam

The car was stuffy and Clare's parents were having another quarrel. They always quarrelled in the car – in the car or in the bathroom. In the car it was always because Mum had lost the way or driven into a traffic jam that was ten miles long. This time it was both. Clare listened as Dad's voice grew louder. Mum gave up the struggle and sank into silence.

"I knew it would be like this," Dad said. His knuckles were white on the steering wheel. "It always is. First you get me lost in Salisbury, and now this traffic. Didn't I tell you we should have taken the other road? Look at it!"

Dad shrugged off his jacket and jerked at the hand-brake again as the car began to roll back. "As if that wasn't enough," he went on, "look at this heat."

"I thought we wanted sun on holiday," Clare said. As soon as the words were out, she regretted that she had opened her mouth. Mum looked round and smiled in understanding.

The traffic started to move again. In the other lane Clare spotted an open sports car. It was white and long and low, and as it drew closer, Clare saw that there was a sweaty-looking man in a silly cowboy hat sitting behind the wheel. She grinned at him as they crawled past, and he grinned back from under his hat and waved at them.

"Blasted show-off!" Dad said under his breath, as he ground the gears. "How far to Exeter? It can't be far now, surely?"

"Not far, dear," Mum said.

"How far? Come on!" Dad snapped.

"Thirty miles or so, maybe less," Mum said.

Dad wouldn't stop. "That's what you said last time," he said.

"You only asked me a mile or so back." There was an edge to Mum's voice now.

'A little longer,' Clare thought, 'and they'll really be at it.'

The seat was sticky under Clare's legs, so she pulled at her skirt, swung her legs onto the seat and curled up. She turned her face into the seat and counted the stitches in the leather, then picked at a thread that had come loose. This was the worst part of the holiday.

Every year for as long as Clare could remember they had spent two weeks of the summer holidays at Great Aunt Dora's cottage in Devon. Clare had a bedroom right up under the thatch of the roof and she could lie in bed in the morning and look out at

the dark line of Dartmoor in the distance. Clare

wondered if that noisy nest of sparrows would still

be there above her head from last year.

The car rumbled on. Dad was still moaning in the front. Clare felt the heat on the back of her neck. Dad's moaning merged with the drone of the engine and she slept.

The car jolted Clare awake. It shuddered, and the engine stopped. She looked up. They were there. Car doors slammed.

Aunty Dora bustled around them, fussing over their suitcases. There was a quick supper of hot tomato soup and cheese on toast, and Clare found herself inside her room and alone. The window was open and Clare could just make out the moors on the darkening horizon. There was no sign of the sparrows' nest in the warm thatch above.

*

Clare had breakfast the next morning with Aunty Dora – the smell of frying bacon and toast had brought her flying down the stairs. Mum and Dad weren't up yet. Aunty Dora pestered her with questions about school.

"When do you go to your next school, dear?" she said, as she sat down on the other side of the table from Clare and sipped her tea noisily.

"I'm already there, Aunty," Clare said. "I've been there for a year now."

"Oh, that's right, dear, of course you have," Aunty Dora said. "And have you got the same boyfriend still? Richard, wasn't it?"

"Robbie, Aunty," Clare said. "His name was Robbie. I haven't seen him for ages."

Aunty Dora was always after gossip and her voice fell to a whisper as she probed for more information about Clare's new boyfriends.

"Peeta's one, then there's Artemis," said Clare.

Aunty Dora nodded and listened as Clare reeled off at least a dozen names from the last six books she'd read. In the end, Aunty Dora began to look shocked. Clare could never make out why she asked so many questions, because she never remembered the answers from one year to the next.

CHAPTER 2
Cow Parsley and Bumble Bees

Clare slammed the door of the cottage behind her.

The sun was hot on her head already and she had the whole morning to herself.

In the sky the swallows and swifts dipped and swooped above the fields. The steep banks that ran along the lanes hummed with life, and now and then the bright colours of a dragonfly or butterfly flashed above the white of the cow parsley. A pair of brown bumble bees dive-bombed Clare at the end of the lane. She climbed the bank and ran down towards the river that rushed and tumbled at the bottom of the hill.

It was still there. Last year, on a day just like this, Clare had bounced a stone seven times across the water before the bounces had dribbled away to nothing and the stone had vanished into the river. She picked up a handful of smooth beach pebbles and tried to beat this record.

The best she could do this morning was three. Disgusted with herself, she hurled a handful of little pebbles that landed in a series of tiny bursts in mid-stream.

Clare turned and ran along the bank. A cross stood a few yards from the river, granite-grey and solemn. She read the words carved on it again.

To the memory of Robert Peverell, aged 14.
Who drowned while fishing in the pool
Near this spot, on 15 August 1897.
May his soul rest in peace.

Clare looked back at the river and tried to picture what had happened. The river didn't look fast in the pool. Did the boy slip? Perhaps someone pushed him.

A wasp bothered Clare and she left the cross and followed the river until she met the lane again.

As Clare clambered down the bank she spotted a lamb further up the lane. It was bleating away and as Clare watched she saw it try to climb first one bank and then the other. Each time the slope was too much, and the lamb toppled back onto the road again.

Clare approached the lamb, careful not to make any sudden movements. The lamb was tired. It ran into the bank as Clare came up and she grabbed it

as it struggled up the impossible slope. She held it to her chest and stroked its head, to try to calm it. She could feel the wild pumping of its heart under her hand. But as Clare walked up and down the lane looking for a gate into the field, the lamb stopped its bleating and struggling.

Clare couldn't find a gate, so she climbed the bank to look for the flock the lamb belonged to. But there was nothing – green fields on both sides, but not an animal in sight. Clare looked around for some clue as to where the lamb came from. Nothing. She walked into the field with the lamb in her arms. She wondered if she should leave it and run off. It might find its way back – but then, it might not.

Far among the trees at the end of the field, Clare thought she saw a wisp of smoke. She ran towards it and as she cleared the rise of the hill she saw the source of the smoke. There was a thatched cottage almost hidden in the fields and the smoke rose in a thin stream from the chimney into the air.

Clare crossed a farmyard where the mud had dried into hard ruts. The cottage was built of the same stuff as Aunt Dora's – a mix of mud and straw they called cob. But where Aunt Dora's cottage was painted white, this one was rusty brown and there were great cracks in it that streaked down the walls. The barn next to the cottage looked as if it were held together by the thatch. That was strange – the thatch was

yellow and new, like a fresh haircut, but the cottage below looked as if one gust of wind could blow it over.

By the time Clare reached the door, she had been joined by chickens and geese that followed her up the path, clucking and hissing at her heels. Clare was a bit worried about the geese, and the lamb must have been as well – it began to struggle again in her arms.

The door opened before Clare could get a hand free to knock.

CHAPTER 3

A Friend of Mine

He was an old man. He stood in front of Clare in a

dirty white shirt with no collar, baggy trousers and

braces. Clare had never seen anyone quite like him.

It wasn't just that his clothes were odd – it was his

face. His hair was white and thin, and a pair of clear

blue eyes sparkled from the creases and lines of his

weather-beaten face.

"That's my lamb you've got there," he said.

Clare felt as if she'd been caught with something she'd stolen. "I found it in the lane," she said. "I didn't know whose it was."

"Where'd you find her, then?" the old man said, and he reached for the lamb.

"Back over there," Clare said. She pointed. "It couldn't climb the bank."

Clare gave the old man the lamb and she was pleased to see that it struggled just as much with him.

"You've my thanks, girl," the old man said. "She's been gone all night. I thought she'd been taken. Come in the house." He led the way out of the sun and into the darkness inside.

"Who would want to take a lamb?" Clare asked, as she squeezed her way into the cluttered room.

"Any number of things, fox, dog, people – you name it, they'd take a lamb."

The old man felt the lamb's back and legs. "She'll be fine," he said, and he put her down on the floor. She bleated and ran off out the back door into the garden on the other side of the house.

The old man stood up straight with the help of the arm of a chair. "Well, girl," he said, "that's half my flock you saved – the other half's her mother. I'm most grateful to you."

Clare looked up into the old man's face and saw his moustache flicker into a smile. "Well, girl," he

said, "sit down if you can find a space. Have a drink –
it's hot enough outside."

"Yes, please," Clare said.

Clare looked around her as the old man went out.
Two tiny windows let in just enough light for her to
make out the far wall of the little room. Every inch of
the wall was covered with pictures, photographs with
curling yellow edges, and old maps. There were the
remains of a hard-boiled egg in a cup and a half-full
carton of milk on the table, along with paint brushes,
paper and several paintings. The chairs were all
used as bookcases, apart from the one by the cooker.
Above the cooker, on the wall above the mantel, was a
painting of a horse in a gold frame.

Clare heard the old man behind her. "Here's your drink, girl," he said.

"Thanks," Clare said. It was water and it was cold and the first taste surprised her – she'd been expecting squash.

"Good?" he asked and she nodded as she drank. "Not from these parts, are you?" he said.

"No," said Clare. "I live in London. I come here for holidays every summer."

"London," he said. "It's a long way to London. I've been there once – long time ago. Before the War. Didn't much like it. Too many people about, too much noise."

Clare was trying to work out his age. If he had fought in World War Two, then he must be over 80 or even 90, she thought.

"There's not much noise here," she said, in between gulps of water.

"No," he said, and he hitched up his braces. "There's the sheep, the stream and Captain. That's about it, and that's how I like it."

"Captain," Clare said. "Who's Captain?"

"Well, girl, since you're a friend of mine, you'll be a friend of his," the old man said. "You'd better meet him. If you've finished that water, come along an' see." He led Clare out of the front door and into the barn.

The old man pointed into the black of the barn. "There he is," he said. "He doesn't like the heat nowadays. Getting on y' know."

Clare heard him before she saw him, and then out of the dark came an old horse still munching away at some hay, which hung out of the sides of his mouth.

"Captain," the old man said, "this is a friend of mine. What's y' name, girl? You haven't told me yet."

"Clare," she said.

"Well, Clare girl, this is Captain," the old man said.

"He's lovely," Clare said. She stroked the white patch on Captain's head.

"Lovely! He's as lovely as I am, girl. But you were handsome enough in your day, weren't you, Captain? Like me, eh?" The old man broke into a fit of laughter that ended in a fit of coughing.

Clare was laughing too – only the horse did not seem amused.

"Captain and me – we've been together now for over 30 year," the old man said. "That right, Captain? Go on, boy, back in your corner, else the flies'll be after you. Ruddy flies."

Captain turned and walked away.

"He's a fine friend," the old man said, as the munching horse disappeared into the darkness again.

"I think he's a lovely old horse," said Clare, looking after him. "Would you let me come and see him again?" She'd asked without really thinking.

"Course you can, girl," said the old man, "and I hope you'll call and see me when you come." He chuckled and held out a wrinkled hand. It was cold and rough, like sandpaper. "My name's Jones, girl, and Captain and me'll be glad to see you."

The old man bowed low. Clare bowed back and ran off up the hill, laughing. At the top of the hill she turned to wave, but the old man was gone.

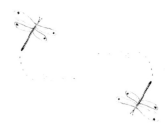

CHAPTER 4

Pork Pie and Cucumber

Lunch was outside, and Mum and Dad and Aunt Dora were already eating when Clare got back. They did not look pleased.

"Where have you been, Clare?" Dad said. His mouth was full of pork pie that Clare could see churning round and round inside.

"You may as well eat now you're here," Aunty Dora said. She poured out some orange juice and Clare wiped her dusty hands on her skirt and sat down.

"Where've you been all this time?" Dad said again.

"I went down to the river," Clare said, as she tried to trap a piece of slithery cucumber on her fork. "And then I found this lamb in the lane, so I took it back to its owner."

"Who was it, dear?" Aunty Dora asked.

"It was an old man called Jones, he lives ..."

"I know where he lives," Aunty Dora said.

It was as if Clare had shouted the dirtiest word she knew.

They had all stopped eating and were looking at each other and then at her.

"Thatcher Jones, was it, dear?" Aunty Dora said, leaning forward.

"I don't know – just Jones, he said."

"Everyone calls him Thatcher," Mum said. "I don't know what his real name is. That was his job, you see, when we were young. Mending thatch."

Clare sat back in her chair while she waited for a wasp to find out her pork pie was not apricot jam. Dad and Aunt Dora were whispering and Mum was looking annoyed.

"How many times have I told you not to talk to strangers, Clare?" Dad was angry now.

"But I had to take ..." Clare tried to explain.

"You heard your father, dear," Aunt Dora joined in.

The one bad thing about the cottage was that Aunt Dora lived there, Clare thought. Aunt Dora meant well, but she got between Mum and Dad and made arguments worse by always supporting Dad.

"Clare," Dad said. "You're not to speak to people you don't know. You know that."

Clare fiddled with the crust on her pork pie, which she didn't want any more.

It was pretty clear Dad and Aunt Dora had something against Thatcher Jones. Well, that was their problem.

That afternoon Mum and Dad took Clare to some
cobbled village by the sea, full of donkeys and poky
little shops. The rest of the world had the same idea –
the place was crammed. From time to time Clare

tried to find out about Thatcher Jones, but Dad just

changed the subject or went on about "strangers".

There was a traffic jam on the way back to the

cottage.

'Just like London,' Clare thought, and she pulled at the loose thread in the back seat and wondered what it was that anyone could possibly have against Thatcher Jones.

CHAPTER 5

A Walk with Captain

Clare was woken the next morning by a family
of sparrows screeching at each other outside her
window. When she leaned out to watch them, they
flew away with angry mutters to each other. She put
on her stripy T-shirt and her blue shorts, and ran
downstairs.

She gulped down a bowl of cornflakes and was down the lane and away before anyone else was up. The stones in the tarmac dug into her bare feet, so she climbed the bank and ran across the field and down past the river again.

Thatcher Jones was feeding the chickens outside the barn when she arrived.

"There's nothing as greedy as a well-fed chicken,"
he said. He watched two rusty red chickens squabble
over a chunk of brown bread. "Nice to see you, girl,"
he said.

"Can I take Captain for a walk?" Clare said. She
stepped back as the chickens made for her toes, their
red crests jerking at the ground close to her feet.

Thatcher Jones puffed at his pipe and sent smoke
signals up into the air in little white clouds. "He'd
like that," he said. "It's been years since he went out.
He spends all his time in the field behind the house or
in the barn."

Captain was grazing in the paddock behind the
house. He looked up as they came over and shook

his head at the flies that were already pestering him.

Clare saw them gathered in great black bunches in

the corners of his eyes.

"Ruddy flies!" Thatcher Jones said, and he waved them away. "It's one thing God should've left out of his plans. Hello, Captain old thing. It's that girl Clare come to take you for a walk." Captain stamped his back legs and swished his tail. "Bit slow getting on your feet this morning, weren't you, old thing?" Thatcher Jones said, as he pulled one of Captain's ears through the bridle straps.

"What's that bump on his nose?" Clare asked.

"That's no bump, girl, that's a beauty spot, isn't it, Captain old thing?" Thatcher Jones said. "It's a big beauty spot, and it may be unusual, but we like it." He laughed and threw the saddle across the horse. "He likes a saddle, y' know, reminds him of his working days. He used to help me, y' know, when I went out and about on my thatching jobs. He used to carry the straw and the reeds. Couldn't have managed without him."

Thatcher Jones handed the reins to Clare. "Take him easy now," he said. "He's not keen on cars either, so mind the lanes."

Captain plodded behind them as they walked across the yard, and Clare felt the reins slack in her hands. "That picture in the gold frame in the cottage," she said. "Is that Captain?"

"That's him," Thatcher Jones said. "I did that years ago now. Your bump wasn't so big then, was it, old thing?"

"You painted him?" Clare asked.

"Long time ago now. Don't see so well now, but I still do a bit every day, keep my hand in." The old man walked away towards the barn. "Don't be too long," he said.

"I'll look after him," Clare said, and she led Captain up the hill and across the field. She took him back towards the river – she thought he'd want a drink after a walk in the sun.

CHAPTER 6

The Mini

Captain didn't like the hard surface of the road.

Whenever he could, he steered into the side and

walked on the grass verge. If he had to tread on the

tarmac, he took very slow and careful steps.

Only once did Clare have any problem with him. The lane went into a steep dip near the river, and Captain slipped on the smooth surface. For a minute or so he wouldn't move at all, until Clare tempted him forwards with handfuls of rich green grass.

When Clare opened the gate into the field by the river, Captain found his feet secure under him again. As they approached the river bank by the cross he almost broke into a trot – but not quite.

Captain lowered his mouth into the river and drank. Clare watched as the old horse used his lower lip to trap the water. As he drank he swished his tail, and Clare wondered if a horse swished his tail for the same reason a dog wags his.

They were on their way back when they met their first car. Captain moved in to the verge and Clare climbed half way up the bank with the reins. The car – a Mini – drove past and stopped a few yards away.

The car doors slammed and Captain looked lazily round. A man and a woman got out. The woman was carrying a large camera.

"Is it your horse?" the woman said.

"No," said Clare. "It belongs to a friend."

"You on holiday here?" the man asked, and he stroked Captain's nose.

"Yes," said Clare, beginning to wonder what it was all about.

"We're from the *South Molton News*," the camera woman said. "Would you mind if we took your photo with the horse?"

"Will it be in the papers?" Clare asked. She was excited at the prospect at seeing herself on the front page.

"This week," the woman said. "If you'll give us your mum or dad's number so we can make sure it's OK. Now you stand there." She turned Clare a little, so that her face was right next to Captain's, and Clare noticed that Captain's teeth were dark yellow – his breath wasn't too good either.

"Give her some grass or something, and look at her," the woman said, as she lined herself up behind her camera. Clare gave the camera a happy smile, and Captain some dried grass which he munched obligingly.

"It's a him," Clare said, "not a her."

"Keep still, love," the woman said. "Thanks very much."

"Can I get your mum's name and phone number, then?" the man said. Clare gave him Aunt Dora's number and told him her own age and where she came from.

"Whose horse is it, love?" the woman asked.

"It's Thatcher Jones's, and his name's Captain," Clare said.

"Thanks, Clare," the man said. "We'll ring tomorrow." And the Mini roared off in a cloud of dust.

"We're going to be famous, Captain," Clare whispered to him as they walked back. But Captain did not look impressed – and neither was Thatcher Jones when she told him.

Before she left Thatcher Jones and Captain, Clare brushed Captain down and hung up his saddle. Thatcher gave her a cool drink of water from the pump outside the barn and she ran off back to the cottage with an invitation to come and visit again tomorrow if she liked. If she liked!

CHAPTER 7

Very Old for a Horse

That afternoon Clare went off for a walk on Dartmoor
with her parents.

She explored a stone circle village, rolled down a
hill on soft, warm heather, and chased a flock of sheep
that did not want anyone to talk to them.

Clare was sitting in the heather after the chase
when it occurred to her that when the people from

the paper rang she would have some explaining to do – so she spent the rest of the day making up a lie that would fit the events.

In the end, Clare disappeared the next morning before anyone else came down, before the newspaper people rang. She was hoping the problem would go away but she knew it wouldn't.

Thatcher Jones's cottage was strangely quiet. The chickens and geese were not there to lead her to the door as usual, and when she knocked on the door, there was no reply. She rubbed the dust off the window and peered into the dark of the sitting room. There was no one there. In the field behind the house there were just the two sheep – no sign of Captain.

The door of the barn was closed and it creaked on its hinges as Clare pushed it open. A shaft of sunlight flooded into the barn.

"Shut the door, girl." It was Thatcher's voice from the darkest corner of the barn, and he sounded old and tired. Clare pushed the door shut, and groped her way towards him.

"What's the matter?" she said, and it was then that she saw Captain lying stretched out on the floor and Thatcher sitting in the straw beside him.

"Come quietly, girl," Thatcher said softly. "Captain's finishing his dying, poor old thing."

"Dying?" Clare said and she held back the choke that welled up into her throat. "He can't be. He was fine yesterday."

"He had a lovely walk," Thatcher said. "He tried to get up when I came in this morning, but he couldn't do it."

Captain took a deep breath every now and again, but his eyes were closed and his great body lay still.

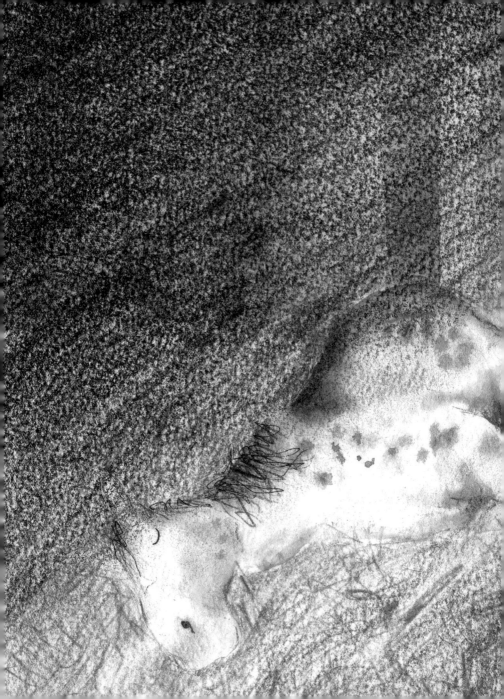

Thatcher looked up at Clare. "He was 35 last year. That's very old for a horse, and you don't have to have a reason to die when you're that old. It just happens," he said. "What I mean, girl, is that your walk yesterday is nothing to do with his dying."

Captain heaved again on the straw.

"Can't we get a vet?" Clare said. "Maybe a vet could help."

"No, Clare girl," Thatcher said. "It'll be over soon. There's nothing can be done."

Clare and the old man watched as Captain tried to lift his head. His eyes flickered open once and his head fell back. He didn't breathe any more.

"Poor old thing," Thatcher said.

Clare could not stop it now. The tears were coming whether she wanted them to or not.

"Anyway, those ruddy flies won't bother him any more," Thatcher Jones said. "Unless there's flies in Heaven, and God couldn't have made that bad a mistake."

"Why are you joking about it?" Clare said, when she could get her breath from her crying.

"Girl," Thatcher said, standing up and putting his arm round her, "there was no one in the world meant more to me than Captain, no one." They walked out into the heat of the day. "He was my only friend for about as long as I care to remember. It'll be lonely without him, but if I started to cry I don't think I could stop. There's the chickens to be fed and life to be lived."

"I'm sorry," Clare managed to say, and she began to run up the hill and away. By the time she reached the river bank she had stopped crying. No matter what Thatcher said, it must have been the walk that finished Captain off. Clare was responsible. There had to be something she could do.

CHAPTER 8

All Bark and No Bite

Dad was in the deck-chair in the garden. Clare hated

seeing him with his shirt off – the fat bulged over his

trousers. He had the newspaper in his hand.

"There you are," he said. "Come here."

Clare walked slowly over. She had forgotten

about the photo and the newspaper, and the last thing

she wanted was to see a picture of Captain.

"Where did you get the horse, Clare?" Dad said.

Aunt Dora and Mum had come out too.

"It's Thatcher Jones's," she said. "He let me take him for a walk."

Dad was out of the chair now and shaking the paper in her face.

"I thought I told you not to talk to him again," Dad said.

Clare wasn't a bit scared. Dad was all bark and no bite.

"No, you didn't," Clare said. "You said I wasn't to talk to strangers."

"Come on, dear." It was Aunt Dora, interfering again. "You know what your father meant."

"He's a friend, not a stranger," Clare said. "I like him, and I'll like who I want to like." She turned and ran indoors and shut herself in her room. Outside she heard angry voices. They were on at Mum for giving permission for the photo to go in the paper. Clare slammed the window with a bang.

At lunch, over Aunt Dora's pasties and half-melted chocolate ice-cream, only Mum spoke to Clare.

And there was a gloomy silence in the car as they drove into South Molton to do some shopping.

Dad broke the silence. "I want to make sure you understand," he said over his shoulder. "You are not to see that man again, and neither will you take his horse out on the roads again. God knows what could have happened. You know nothing about horses."

"What's wrong with Thatcher Jones?" Clare asked.

"Nothing's wrong with him," Dad said. "You're not to go back there. That's all."

"Thatcher Jones is a recluse, Clare," Mum said. "He's a kind of hermit, and because he lives alone and keeps to himself, people think he's strange. That's why they don't want you to see him."

Dad and Aunt Dora said nothing.

"Isn't that right?" Mum went on. "It's nothing to do with strangers. Clare knows fine well she's not to talk to strangers. But she's got a right to make her own friends."

Clare smiled and then she saw Dad looking at her in the rear-view mirror.

Clare picked up the newspaper which Dad had thrown onto the back seat. There was the photo, and underneath it she read the caption – "Clare and her Captain".

She looked at her face and straggly hair in the photo. It looked as if she shared the same mane as Captain. She wanted to tell Mum about Captain, but every time she thought about it a lump came into her throat, and anyway Aunt Dora was in the car and Clare couldn't say anything while she was there.

They had only been in the market a few minutes before Clare had had enough. People were pushing

and shoving, the market smelled of fish, and an old
man stepped on her toes.

"Can I wait outside?" Clare asked her mum. Mum
nodded and Clare fled.

As Clare walked out, she saw "South Molton News"
in big green letters over a doorway across the street.

Whether it was that, or the brown and white horse that was being led by, that put the idea into her head, she didn't know – but all of a sudden she saw a way of softening the blow of Captain's death for Thatcher Jones. A way of making up for what she had done.

CHAPTER 9

Everything to Him

Clare pushed open the door and walked in. There was a girl sitting at a long desk – she looked bored and fed up and she was filing her finger nails. They were olive-green.

She didn't bother to look up. "Yes?" she said.

"Can I see the manager?" Clare said.

"You mean the Editor." The girl sighed.

"The person in charge," Clare said. She was beginning to be annoyed.

"What do you want to see him about?" The girl looked up from her green nails. "Wait a minute," she said. "You're the girl in the photo with the horse." Clare nodded. "Do you want a copy? Is that it? It's 65p, you know."

"No thanks," Clare said. The door banged behind her. She turned and recognised the man who had been with the woman when they'd taken her picture in the lane.

"Please, sir!" Clare said as he walked past.

He knew her at once and took her through a noisy office and into the peace of a small, cluttered room.

She saw the words "Editor – Charlie Simmonds" on a sign on the door. He cleared some papers off a chair.

"Are you the Editor?" Clare asked. He nodded.

"Sit down," he said. "Did you like the photo? You can have a copy if you like."

"It's about something else," Clare said, and she sat on the edge of her chair and told him everything that had happened and how she knew it was her fault.

"There's only one way I can make it up to Thatcher Jones," she said. "I must find another horse for him. I thought you could help."

"It's very difficult, you know, just to find a horse. I mean, they cost money." Mr Simmonds pushed his chair back on its back legs and tapped his nose with a pencil.

"I think he'll die without something," Clare said. "He had Captain for over 30 years. There must be someone with an old horse they don't want."

"I don't know, Clare. People get fond of horses, and anyway, how do you know he'll want a different horse?" Mr Simmonds said. "It sounds to me as if Captain was rather special to him."

"He'll be lonely," Clare said. "Mum says he's a hermit or something, nobody seems to like him and he never sees anyone. Captain was everything to him."

Mr Simmonds rocked his chair forward, threw down his pencil and typed something into his laptop.

"All right, Clare," he said. "I think I know someone who might help. No promises, mind." He dialled a number. "I'll meet you in the lane, same place, six o'clock this evening. Bring your mum or dad along. Off you go now."

"Thank you," said Clare. She couldn't think of anything else to say and anyway Mr Simmonds was already talking on the phone. On the way out, she saw that the girl at the desk was still filing her green nails.

The car journey on the way back was even worse. Clare had promised to wait outside the market, but instead she'd wandered off without letting them know.

Dad and Aunt Dora were hopping mad. It was sheer luck, Dad said, sheer luck they'd found her back at the car. Mum sat next to Clare in the back and a kind of iron curtain of silence was drawn between the front and the back seats.

Tea was even more tense. Dad moaned on about "young people today".

By half past five, Clare couldn't wait any longer.

"Can I go out?" she asked. "I'll be home for supper."

Dad was about to say no, but then Mum said she

fancied a walk too and they escaped together.

CHAPTER 10
Two Long Ears

Mum walked at a snail's pace but Clare ran along the

river banks, dodging clouds of midges and swiping at

them as she ran past. The lane was deserted, so she

sat down in the cow parsley by the side of the road

and waited. The tarmac shimmered with the heat. It

was like a sheet of glass at the end of the lane.

Clare heard the crunch of tyres on the road. The Mini drew up, trailing a horse box. Mr Simmonds rolled down his window.

"Take a look, Clare," he said. "See what you think."

Clare pulled at the top of the tail board to help herself jump up behind the horse box. There was a horsey smell, but the shaggy brown bottom that faced her did not belong to any horse. Further into the box, a head turned to investigate her. Then two long ears pricked up and Clare knew what she was seeing.

"A donkey!" said Mum, who had arrived at last.

"Well, what do you think?" Mr Simmonds said.

Clare did not know what to think. A donkey's not quite the same as a horse. "Where did you get him?" she asked.

"He's a her," Mr Simmonds said, and Clare grinned at him. She was beginning to like the idea.

"I rang up the Donkey Rest Home place," he said. "This one's about 18 years old, and as gentle as you like."

"He's a bit shaggy," Clare said as they helped the donkey down – you could hardly see her eyes for the hair. "I don't know whether Thatcher Jones will like him."

"Her," Mr Simmonds said. "Let's find out."

CHAPTER 11

Tea

Thatcher Jones came out of his cottage and puffed on his pipe as Mr Simmonds and Mum walked the donkey down the hill towards him. Clare ran on ahead.

"What've you got there, girl?" Thatcher said as she came up.

"She's yours, Thatcher. It's a donkey. We couldn't find a real horse," Clare said. And then for the first time she wondered whether it was too soon, too sudden a change for Thatcher to accept.

"Mine, girl?" Thatcher said. "And who's this, then?" he asked, with a nod at Mr Simmonds and Mum.

"This is my mum," Clare said. "And the man who put the photo in the paper. I told you about it."

"I hope you like her," Mr Simmonds said, and he handed the donkey's reins to Thatcher. "Clare wanted a horse, but this was the best we could find."

"Has she got a name, girl?" Thatcher said, as he patted the donkey's dusty neck.

"No," said Mr Simmonds. "I don't think so."

"I like 'Clare', don't you?" Thatcher said to
Mr Simmonds. "You take her out to the field and
introduce her to the sheep, girl, and then we'll have a
cup of tea." He led the donkey over to Clare and gave
her the reins. "That was a nice thing you done, girl,"
he said. "You'll come and help look after her, eh?"

Clare nodded and looked away.

"Look at them ruddy flies," Thatcher Jones said, brushing them off the donkey's face. "Come on in, then," he said to Mr Simmonds and Mum. "We can leave it to her. I've not had anyone to tea for a long, long time," he said. "Must be more than 30 years."

The Story of Clare and her Captain

When I was young I used to spend my Easter holidays with Peggy and Sean, who kept a pub in Devon. Their daughter, Christian, and I loved horses. So when Mr Jones the Thatcher – his job was to thatch roofs with reeds or rushes – said we could take Captain, his old horse, for walks round the lanes, we were thrilled. We always went with Velvet the dog and took it in turns to ride Captain.

One morning it was my turn. I was leading Captain, trying to find a gate to climb up and get on. Christian and Velvet had walked on ahead and I was alone with Captain. A car drew up beside us and two men got out and asked if they could take a picture of me and Captain together.

"Of course," I said.

They took some pictures, asked me some questions and drove off. I scrambled onto Captain and we trotted up the lane to catch up with Christian and Velvet. The next day the photo was in the *Western Morning News*. I was famous for a day, and so was my Captain!

Many years later, this little story inspired Michael to write this book.

Clare Morpurgo